The Princess of 5th Avenue

For Frankie

The Princess of 5th Avenue

Amy Weber

New Lady Publishing

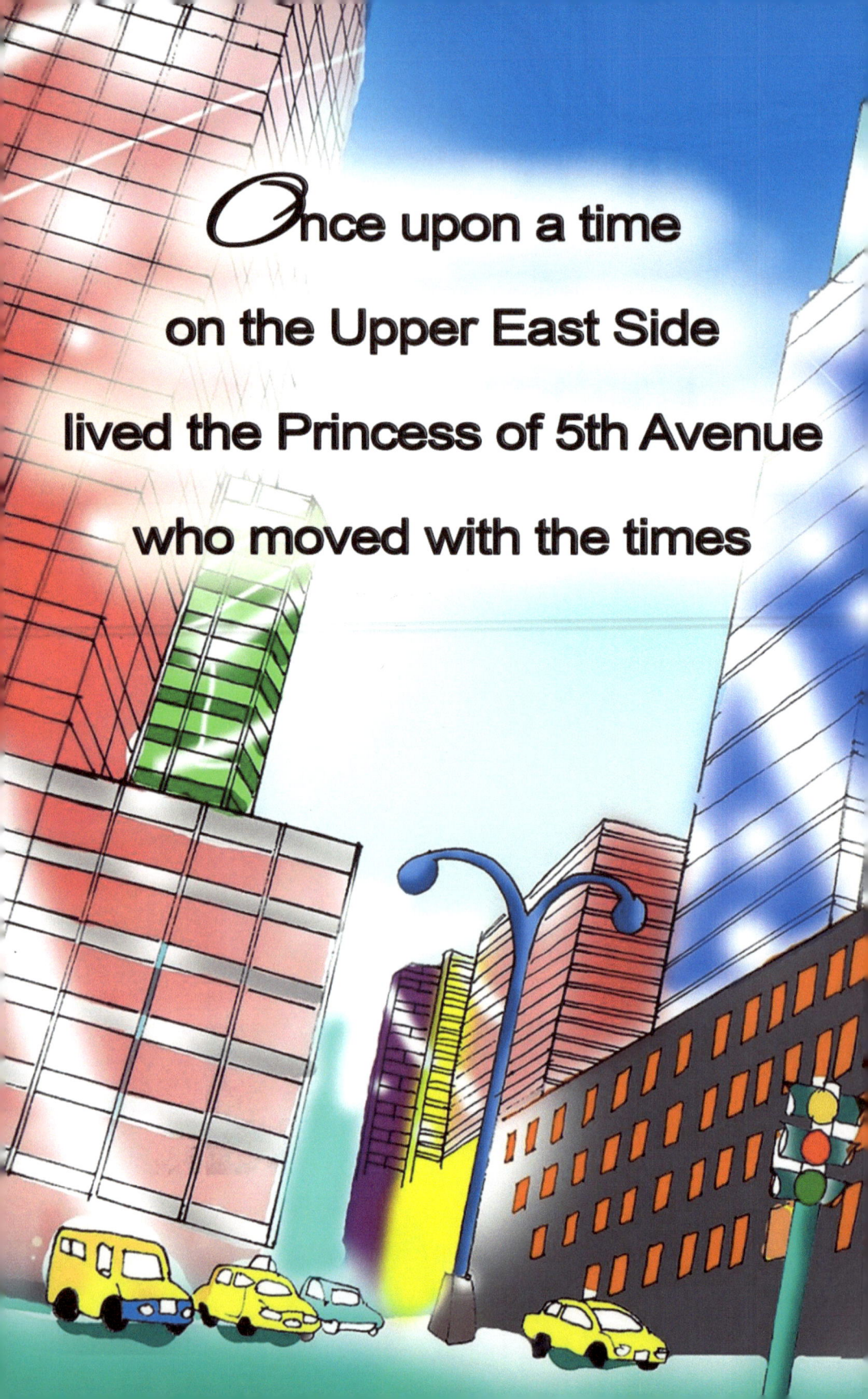

Once upon a time

on the Upper East Side

lived the Princess of 5th Avenue

who moved with the times

Her name was Isabella

her locks always curled

her shoes always shined

She was born to rule the world

She lived with her Mommy

who wore lots of jewels

as well as her Daddy

and their scruffy mutt Drools

Each morning she woke

to the view of the Park

the smell of french toast

and the sound of Drools' bark

Dressed in Dior

Jimmy Choo on her feet

the Princess would lunch

with her Daddy on Wall Street

When her belly was full

from the Wall Street Cafe

to Barneys she went

She was Manhattan savvy

The girls whispered and giggled

on the grand seventh floor

the view of Central Park

made them giggle some more

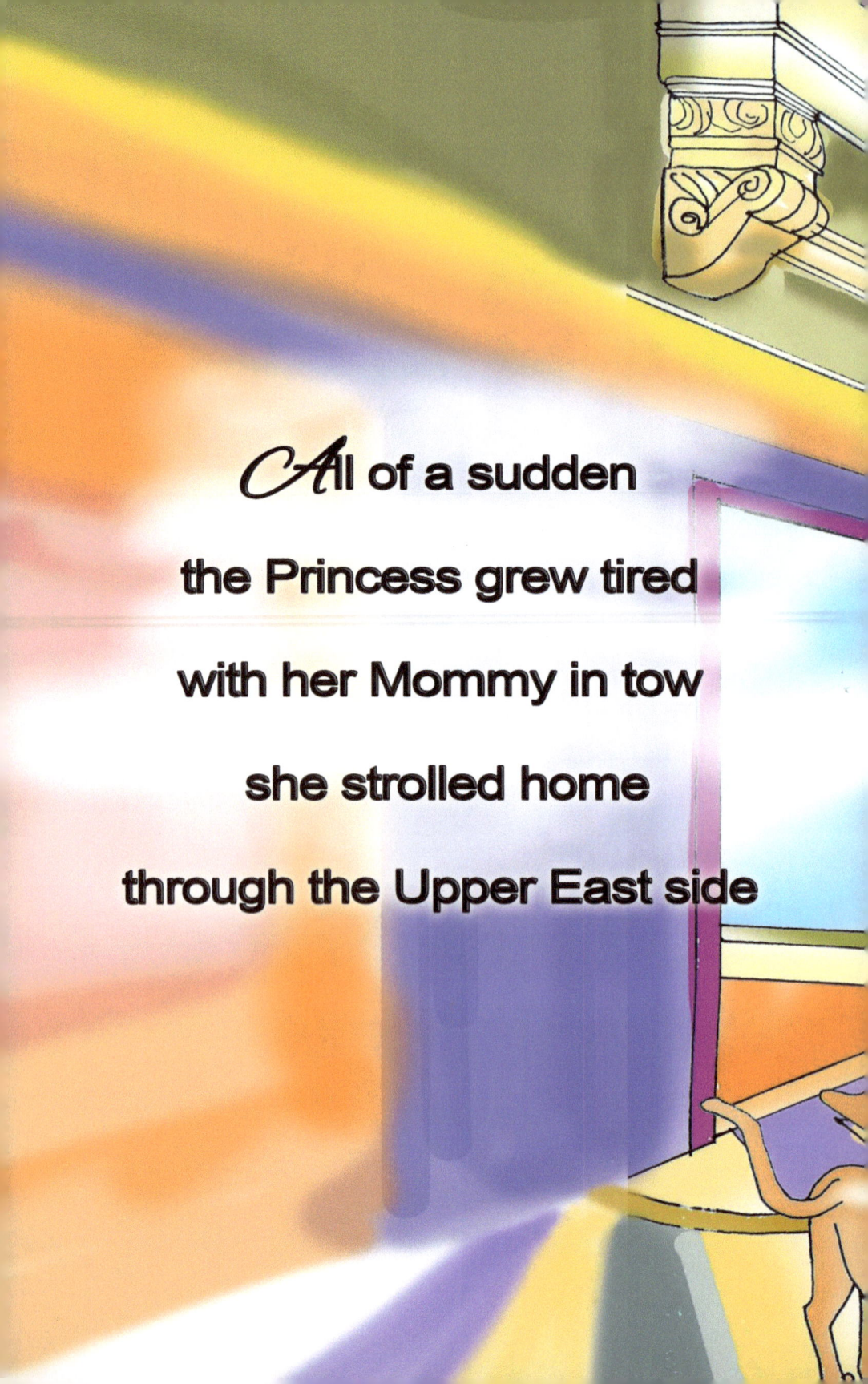

All of a sudden

the Princess grew tired

with her Mommy in tow

she strolled home

through the Upper East side

In fairy pajamas

"I love you" she heard

She pulled down her mask

Please do not disturb

www.ingramcontent.com/pod-product-compliance
Lightning Source LLC
Chambersburg PA
CBHW040901120626
46551CB00001B/121